Louie loves to play

Yves Got

In the park,
Louie loves playing on
the slide.

F

First published in Great Britain in 2002
by Zero To Ten Limited
327 High Street, Slough,
Berkshire, SL1 1TX

Copyright © Yves Got 2000
English text by Simona Sideri
copyright © 2002 Zero to Ten Limited
Originally published under the title of
DIDOU aime jouer
by Albin Michel Inc., France, in 2000
All rights reserved.

A CIP catalogue record for this book is available from the British Library.

ISBN 1-84089-247-1

Printed and bound in Asia

He makes HUGE
sandcastles.

He meets
his friend, Annie.
"I like your car,"
he says.

Louie always has a ride on the merry-go-round.

Wheeeeeee!
Louie and croc are off
on an adventure!

The park is
the best place
to play hide and seek.

Louie makes a huge pile of leaves and puts them in the bin.

"Don't worry Teddy," says Louie.
"We can play again
when it stops raining."

Louie likes to have a carrot lolly
when it's time to go home.

Louie loves cars
ISBN 1-84089 246-3

Louie loves his little sister
ISBN 1-84089 248-X

Louie loves to play
ISBN 1-84089 247-1

Louie loves a cuddle
ISBN 1-84089 249-8

Join the Louie Club!

Look out for all the Louie books... and lots of other fantastic titles for babies and toddlers – from Zero to Ten!

ZERO TO TEN books are available from all good bookstores. If you have any problems obtaining any title, or to order a catalogue or join our mailing list, please contact the publishers:
ZERO TO TEN LTD., 327 High Street, Slough, Berkshire SL1 1TX
Tel: 01753 578 499 Fax: 01753 578 488